Brother Aelred's Feet

Quiz No 213055
Brother Aelred's Feet

Cross, Gillian
B.L.: 4.0
Points: 0.5　　　　MY

D1422092

Written by Gillian Cross

Illustrated by Tim Stevens

⦿ Collins

Chapter 1

If Brother Aelred stepped into the dairy, the milk turned sour. If he helped in the kitchen, the meat went rotten. If he walked through the vegetable garden, next day's soup tasted of old socks.

Aelred had the smelliest feet in the whole ninth century. Anywhere. And he was the only person who couldn't smell them.

Apart from that, he was an ideal monk. He was plump and humble and very short, but he could sing like an angel. And when he copied manuscripts, he filled them with tiny, beautiful pictures. If it hadn't been for his feet ...

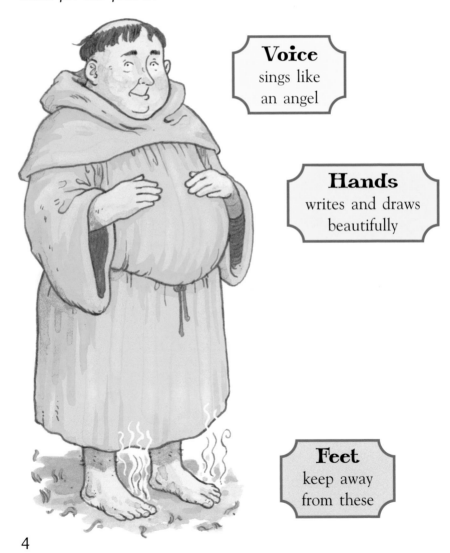

Voice
sings like
an angel

Hands
writes and draws
beautifully

Feet
keep away
from these

... but his feet were impossible.

At last, the old Abbot had an idea. He called Aelred into his cell. "Brother," he said, "I have a job for you."

Aelred beamed. "In the writing room, Father? Copying the holy books?"

The Abbot thought of Aelred's beautiful manuscripts. Then he thought of the cramped, airless room where the monks sat copying out the gospels and the service books.

"Not the writing room," he said gently.

Aelred's face fell. Then he brightened. "What about the choir? I love singing psalms in Saint Meregonda's Chapel."

The Abbot remembered Aelred's fine tenor voice. But he also remembered the tiny, windowless chapel where Saint Meregonda's relics lay. "I was thinking of a more open-air job," he said. "How do you feel about ... pigs?"

"Pigs?"

The monastery pigs were wild and hairy and ugly. But Aelred was a humble man. He knelt and kissed the Abbot's ring.

"Thank you, Father," he said. "I'll take good care of the pigs."

And he did. Every morning, he drove them up the hill behind the monastery. He stayed there all day, praying and singing, while the pigs grunted and rooted for acorns.

Chapter 2

The pigs didn't mind Aelred's feet. In fact, they
rather liked the smell. They liked his singing, too.
And they loved Aelred himself, because he looked
after them so well.

When he had finished singing, Aelred collected pieces of bark and decorated them with pictures of Saint Meregonda, colouring them with berries and leaves and roots.

That was what he was doing when the Vikings came. He had just finished drawing Saint Meregonda's dragon when he glimpsed something fluttering in the bay beyond the hill. Looking down, he saw a longship anchored off the shore. Huge warriors were leaping out of it, with battle-axes in their hands.

Aelred didn't waste a second. Tucking the bark picture into his belt, he raced down to the monastery, shouting at the top of his voice.

"Vikings! Vikings!"

The pigs followed him, squealing shrilly, and they all crashed through the front gate of the monastery.

"Vikings!" Aelred yelled. "The Vikings have landed in the bay!"

All the other monks came hurrying out of their cells. Their faces were white. They knew how the Vikings smashed and looted and pillaged.

Only the old Abbot was calm. "We can hide in the forest," he said. "But we must save our treasures. Who will take them across the causeway to the mainland?"

There was a terrible, terrified silence. Even the pigs stopped oinking.

The Abbot frowned. "We can't let the Vikings capture our holy books and the relics of Saint Meregonda. Will no one save them?"

Aelred stepped forward. "I will," he said.

Aelred? No one could believe it. He was much too small to fight off any Vikings.

But the old Abbot smiled at him. "God gives us all different gifts. Maybe he will use yours now, Brother Aelred. Let us hurry."

Chapter 3

Monks raced off in all directions, tripping over the pigs as they went. Out came the big wooden chest from the church. Saint Meregonda's relics and the holy books were packed into it and it was lifted on to the monastery's donkey cart.

When the pigs saw Aelred leaving with the cart, they tried to follow him, but the monks drove them back and shut them into the barn. They grunted miserably as they heard Aelred and the donkey marching away.

He was just out of sight when the Vikings came howling over the hill, brandishing axes and bellowing threats. The monks took one look and raced into the forest. By the time the Vikings reached the monastery, it was deserted.

The Viking leader was a wild giant of a man called Erik. He smashed down the monastery gate and charged in, shouting at his men.

"ATTACK!"

They followed, with their axes waving, but there was no one to attack. Erik glared round.

"LOOT AND PILLAGE!" he yelled.

The Vikings ransacked the monastery buildings.
There were no treasures. No monks. But when they
opened the barn doors, out galloped a herd of wild,
hairy pigs, snorting angrily.

Erik hadn't been expecting pigs. He had seventeen brothers, all bigger and fiercer than he was, and he wanted some rare and precious treasure to impress them. But pigs were better than nothing.

"SEIZE THEM!" he bellowed.

The Vikings tried, but the pigs had different ideas. They dodged and doubled and darted, heading for the gate. They didn't want to be seized. They wanted to follow Aelred.

"AFTER THEM!" raged Erik.

19

Chapter 4

Down the road streamed the pigs, squealing and grunting, with the Vikings pelting in chase. Aelred was safely out of sight, but the pigs knew exactly where he'd gone. They charged after him.

A mile ahead, Aelred heard the noise and he was terrified. He didn't know what was going on, but he tugged at the donkey's bridle, trying to make it go faster. That was a mistake. The donkey planted its feet firmly in the mud, and refused to move.

Aelred wanted to run, but he couldn't leave the holy relics and the precious books. And the wooden chest was too heavy to move. In desperation, he opened the lid and squeezed inside the chest himself. Pulling the lid down, he lay as still as he could.

It wasn't a great plan. When the pigs eventually
reached the cart, they crowded joyfully round it, oinking
at the chest. The Vikings thundered up behind and
Erik's eyes gleamed. His instinct told him that there
was something very special inside that chest.
The kind of thing he needed to impress his brothers.

"PILLAGE!" he yelled.

Two massive Vikings leapt forward and began to tug at the lid of the chest. The others crowded round, eager to see what treasures were inside. Wedged in between the books and the relics, Aelred clutched desperately at the rim of the lid, holding it shut.

But he didn't stand a chance. More and more Vikings grabbed it, heaving hard.

"GET IT OPEN, YOU WEAKLINGS!" Erik was bellowing.

The Vikings tugged until their faces went purple,
and Aelred's fingers slipped and lost their grip.
With a crash, the lid of the box flew open ...

... and out flooded the smell of Aelred's feet.

They'd been shut inside the chest for almost half an hour. The smell was ripe and rich and it hit the Vikings full on. They staggered backwards, swayed dizzily – and passed out.

Cautiously, Aelred sat up and looked round. What was going on? He was surrounded by unconscious Vikings and wild, hairy pigs.

When the pigs saw him, they went berserk with joy. Oinking and squealing, they charged up to him, pushing their snouts against his robe and chewing his fingers.

"Peace," said Aelred.

But the pigs were too excited to stop. The squealing got louder and louder. Aelred did the only thing he knew that calmed them down.

He started to sing.

Chapter 5

He was still singing when the Vikings opened their eyes.
One by one, they sat up and looked round, wondering
who'd knocked them out. They were expecting to see a
giant or an army of English soldiers. But there was no
one there, except a little fat monk sitting in a wooden
box, singing like an angel. All round the box were wild,
hairy pigs, gazing up adoringly at him.

The Vikings were terrified. They thought Aelred was a wizard.

Erik was the last man to come round. He had been nearest to the chest and caught the full blast of Aelred's feet. He didn't remember exactly what had happened because he'd hit his head on the ground, but he could see there was something extraordinary going on. He was amazed to find himself trembling.

"WHO ARE YOU?" he yelled at Aelred.

Aelred didn't understand the language of the Vikings, but he saw that Erik was confused and afraid.

"Peace," he said soothingly. Exactly as he said it to the pigs. He felt silly sitting in the box, so he started to climb out, singing gently. He sang the pigs' favourite song.

"Pa-a-ax vo-bi-is-cum."

Erik was even more afraid. He thought it was a spell. Jumping up, he seized his axe, ready to chop Aelred into pieces if he came any closer. All the other Vikings watched in terror. They were sure that Aelred was a magician and that he would blast them with lightning if Erik attacked him. But they were frightened of Erik as well. They didn't know what to do.

"Pa-a-ax vo-bi-is-cum," sang Aelred soothingly, jumping down from the cart. Up went Erik's axe, ready for the death blow. But at the last moment, just before the axe fell, something flapped at Aelred's waist. A piece of bark tucked into his belt. Erik glimpsed lines and marks on it, and he stepped back.

"MAGIC!" he shouted.

Aelred didn't understand, but he saw Erik looking at the bark. "Peace," he said again. Smiling, he pulled the bark from his belt and held it out.

Erik reached out nervously and took it. Looking down, he saw a small, bright picture of a woman leading a fierce-looking dragon. He didn't know anything about Saint Meregonda, so he was certain that the bark was a magic charm. A rare and precious treasure to impress his seventeen brothers.

He knelt down and bowed to Aelred. It's always
sensible to keep on good terms with magicians.

Then he leapt up and started giving orders. To Aelred's
amazement, the other Vikings all bowed too.
They began to march away up the road, singing
Aelred's song.

"Pa-a-ax vob-i-is-cum ..."

Chapter 6

Aelred waited for a long time, until the sound of
singing had died away completely. Then he picked up
the donkey's bridle and began to lead it back to the
monastery, with the pigs trotting along behind.

The other monks came out of hiding. They were standing at the top of the hill, watching the Viking longship sail away. When they saw Aelred, they ran down the hill to meet him.

"Well done, Brother!" said the Abbot. "The Vikings came to loot and pillage, but you have sent them away singing about peace."

Aelred was baffled. "What did I do?"

The monks couldn't tell him, but they stood and cheered. Then they led him into the church, for a service of thanksgiving. Afterwards, the Abbot took him aside.

"You deserve a reward, Brother," he said. "Would you like to work in the writing room?"

Aelred thought about it. Then he thought about the pigs.

"Thank you, Father," he said. "I can't leave the pigs. But I should like to work in the writing room in the winter, when it's too dark to go into the woods."

So that is what he did. In summer, he looked after the pigs, and in winter he copied manuscripts, drawing lovely pictures in the margins of the holy books.

Summer

Winter

After a while, the other monks began to notice how pleasant the writing room smelt in winter. "Like incense and roses," they said.

It took them a long time to realise that it was the smell of Brother Aelred's feet ...

A character web

Brother
Aelred

Humble
Aelred doesn't mind looking after the pigs.

Observant
He was the first person to spot the Vikings invading.

Brave
Aelred offers to protect the holy books and relics during the Viking invasion.

Talented
His drawing of Saint Meregonda makes the Vikings believe he is a magician.

Calm
The Vikings leave singing Aelred's song of peace.

Ideas for guided reading

Learning objectives: identify the main characteristics of the key characters, drawing on the text to justify views, and using the information to predict actions; explore narrative order: identify and map out the main stages of the story; identify the use of powerful verbs; respond appropriately to the contribution of others in the light of alternative viewpoints

Curriculum links: History: Why have people invaded and settled in Britain in the past? A Viking case study; PE: Invasion games; RE: What do signs and symbols mean in religion?

Interest words: monk, century, humble, manuscripts, gospels, psalms, tenor, relics, monastery, rooted, pillage, brandishing, ransacked, seized, pelting, unconscious, berserk, adoringly

Resources: whiteboard, pens, paper, poster-sized paper

Getting started

This book can be read over two guided reading sessions.

- Introduce the title and use the interest words to activate children's prior knowledge or to introduce the character and setting.

- Introduce the main character by reading pp2-4 together. Discuss the meaning of the word *humble* and check that the group understands what a manuscript is.

- Discuss Brother Aelred's problem and make predictions. *Can the children predict how others will treat Brother Aelred and how he will react?*

Reading and responding

- As they read, the children should be thinking about the main stages of a narrative and how the events fit into these stages.

- Ask them to make 4 columns with the headings: introduction, build up, crisis, end. As they read, they should record the events under the appropriate heading.